A Note to Parents and Caregivers:

Read-it! Joke Books are for children who are moving ahead on the amazing road to reading. These fun books support the acquisition and extension of reading skills as well as a love of books.

Published by the same company that produces *Read-it!* Readers, these books introduce the question/answer and dialogue patterns that help children expand their thinking about language structure and book formats.

When sharing joke books with a child, read in short stretches. Pause often to talk about the meaning of the jokes. The question/answer and dialogue formats work well for this purpose and provide an opportunity to talk about the language and meaning of the jokes. Have the child turn the pages and point to the pictures and familiar words. When you read the jokes, have fun creating the voices of characters or emphasizing some important words. Be sure to reread favorite jokes.

There is no right or wrong way to share books with children. Find time to read with your child, and pass on the legacy of literacy.

Adria F. Klein, Ph.D.
Professor Emeritus
California State Universi
San Bernardino, Californ

Editor: Christianne Jones
Designer: Joe Anderson
Page Production: Melissa Kes
Art Director: Keith Griffin
Managing Editor: Catherine Neitge
The illustrations in this book were prepared digitally.

Picture Window Books
5115 Excelsior Boulevard
Suite 232
Minneapolis, MN 55416
877-845-8392
www.picturewindowbooks.com

Library of Congress Cataloging-in-Publication Data
Ziegler, Mark, 1954-
School kidders : a book of school jokes / written by Mark Ziegler;
illustrated by Anne Haberstroh.
p. cm.– (Read-it! joke books–supercharged!)
ISBN 1-4048-0964-3
1. Schools–Juvenile humor. 2. Education–Juvenile humor. 3. Riddles,
Juvenile. I. Haberstroh, Anne. II. Title. III. Series.

PN6231.S3Z54 2004
818'.602–dc22   2004018430

School Kidders

A Book of School Jokes

By Mark Ziegler • Illustrated by Anne Haberstroh

Reading Advisers:

Adria F. Klein, Ph.D.
Professor Emeritus, California State University
San Bernardino, California

Susan Kesselring, M.A., Literacy Educator
Rosemount-Apple Valley-Eagan (Minnesota) School District

PICTURE WINDOW BOOKS
Minneapolis, Minnesota

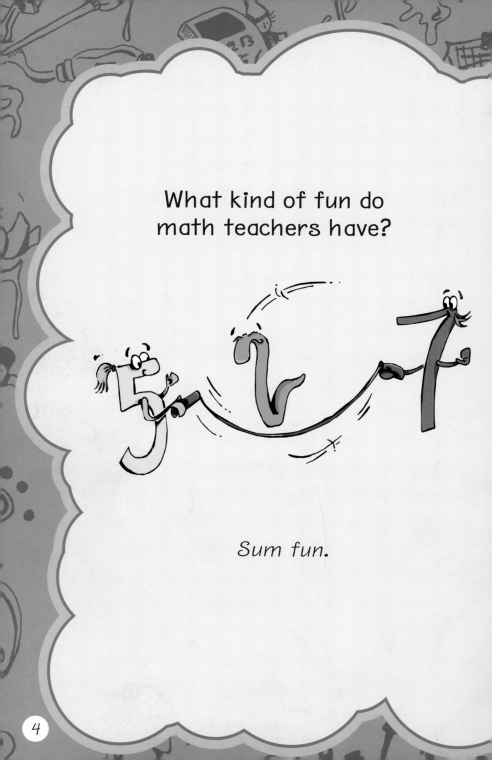

Mom: "How do you like your astronomy class?"

Son: "It's looking up."

How do you make a bandstand?

Hide all their chairs.

What do music teachers give their students?

Sound advice.

What do you call a
duck that always
gets good grades?

A wise quacker.

What did one math book say
to the other math book?

"Boy, do I have problems!"

Why was the school library
so tall?

Because it had so many stories.

Why did the thermometer go to school?

It wanted to gain a degree.

Why were the students all bruised?

Their class went on a trip.

Did the little tornado pass its math test?

Yeah. It was a breeze.

What did the teacher do with the cheese's homework?

She grated it.

Why did the student eat a dollar bill?

His mother told him it was for lunch.

What's big, yellow, and makes parents happy?

The school bus.

Why did the girl bring a jump rope to math class?

So she could skip the test.

Why did the boy eat his spelling test?

His teacher said it was a piece of cake.

Why was the jungle cat thrown out of school?

He was a cheetah.

Why did the girl put on lipstick in class?

The teacher was giving a make-up exam.

Why didn't the bird try out for the diving team?

Because he was a chicken.

Why did the girls wear swimsuits to school?

They rode in a car pool.

School Nurse: "Have your eyes ever been checked?"

Student: "No. They've always been blue."

Why did the student swallow all his pennies?

The teacher said he needed more sense.

What was the snake's favorite class?

Hisssssss-story.

Teacher: "The answer to the math question is zero."

Student: "All that work for nothing!"

Why did the math teacher take a ruler to bed?

She wanted to see how long she slept.

How are elementary teachers like farmers?

They both help little things grow.

What was the witch's favorite subject in school?

Spelling.

What animal makes the best teacher?

A skunk because it makes the most scents.

Why did the nurse fail art class?

He could only draw blood.

Who keeps track of all the meals in the school cafeteria?

The lunch counter.

Teacher: "Does anyone know which month has 28 days?"

Student: "All of them."

Why did the girl bring a ladder to class?

Because she was starting high school.

What kind of pliers does a math
teacher use?
Multipliers.

Teacher: "Why does the Statue
of Liberty stand in the New
York Harbor?"

Student: "Because it can't
sit down."

What runs all around the school
without moving?
The fence.

Teacher: "Do you know the 20th
president of the United States?"

Student: "No. We were never
introduced."

Why did the teacher pour glue on the student's head?

To help things stick to her mind.

What kind of tree does a math teacher climb?

A geometry.

Who should be your best friend at school?

Your princi-pal!

Teacher: "Why is the Mississippi such an unusual river?"

Student: "Because it has four eyes and still can't see."

Why is six afraid of seven?

Because seven ate nine.

Teacher: "Why are you standing on your head?"

Student: "I'm just turning things over in my mind."

Where does success come before work?

In the dictionary.

Teacher: "Why are you reading the last pages of your history book first?"

Student: "I want to know how it ends."

What has 40 feet and sings?

The school choir.

Why was the math book unhappy?

Because it had so many problems.

Read-it! Joke Books— Supercharged!

Beastly Laughs: A Book of Monster Jokes by Michael Dahl

Chalkboard Chuckles: A Book of Classroom Jokes by Mark Moore

Creepy Crawlers: A Book of Bug Jokes by Mark Moore

Critter Jitters: A Book of Animal Jokes by Mark Ziegler

Giggle Bubbles: A Book of Underwater Jokes by Mark Ziegler

Goofballs! A Book of Sports Jokes by Mark Ziegler

Lunchbox Laughs: A Book of Food Jokes by Mark Ziegler

Roaring with Laughter: A Book of Animal Jokes by Michael Dahl

School Kidders: A Book of School Jokes by Mark Ziegler

Sit! Stay! Laugh! A Book of Pet Jokes by Michael Dahl

Spooky Sillies: A Book of Ghost Jokes by Mark Moore

Wacky Wheelies: A Book of Transportation Jokes by Mark Ziegler

Looking for a specific title or level? A complete list of *Read-it!* Readers is available on our Web site: *www.picturewindowbooks.com*